TAMPA BAY BUCCANEERS

BY ALEX MONNIG

Published by The Child's World®
1980 Lookout Drive • Mankato, MN 56003-1705
800-599-READ • www.childsworld.com

Acknowledgments
The Child's World®: Mary Berendes, Publishing Director
Red Line Editorial: Editorial direction
The Design Lab: Design
Amnet: Production

Design Element: Dean Bertoncelj/Shutterstock Images
Photographs ©: Tom DiPace/AP Images, cover; Jeff
Haynes/AP Images for Panini, 5; Phelan M. Ebenhack/AP
Images, 7, 11; NFL Photos/AP Images, 9; Scott A. Miller/AP
Images, 13; Scott Iskowitz/AP Images, 14-15; John A.
Angelillo/Corbis, 17; Arthur Anderson/AP Images, 19;
Thomas O'Neill/NurPhoto/Corbis, 21; Matt Brown/
NewSport/Corbis, 23; Don Kelly Photo/Corbis, 25; Mark
LoMoglio/Icon Sportswire/Corbis, 27; Reuters/Corbis, 29

ISBN 9781634070140
LCCN 2014959719

Printed in the United States of America
Mankato, MN
July, 2015
PA02265

ABOUT THE AUTHOR

Alex Monnig is a freelance journalist from St. Louis, Missouri, who now lives in Sydney, Australia. He has traveled across the world to cover sporting events in China, India, Singapore, New Zealand, and Scotland. No matter where he is, he always makes time to keep up to date with his favorite teams from his hometown.

TABLE OF CONTENTS

GO, BUCCANEERS

The Tampa Bay Buccaneers have seen the highs and lows of football. They lost their first 26 games. And they have the lowest winning percentage of any current team. But it has not been all bad. Tampa Bay won the **Super Bowl** after the 2002 season. Fans get pumped up during years in which "the Bucs" make the playoffs. Let's meet the Buccaneers.

Buccaneers wide receiver Vincent Jackson catches a pass against the Green Bay Packers on December 21, 2014.

WHO ARE THE BUCCANEERS?

The Tampa Bay Buccaneers play in the National Football **League** (NFL). They are one of the 32 teams in the NFL. The NFL includes the American Football Conference (AFC) and the National Football Conference (NFC). The winner of the AFC plays the winner of the NFC in the Super Bowl. The Buccaneers play in the South Division of the NFC. They have played in one Super Bowl. Tampa Bay beat the Oakland Raiders after the 2002 season.

Buccaneers running back Doug Martin runs with the ball against the New Orleans Saints on December 28, 2014.

WHERE THEY CAME FROM

The Buccaneers entered the NFL in 1976. The team was named in a fan contest. There were more than 400 entries. Team owner Hugh Culverhouse picked Buccaneers. That's what pirates who roamed the Caribbean were called. Tampa Bay did not win until the 13th game of its second year. But it made the playoffs after the 1979, 1981, and 1982 seasons. The Bucs had losing seasons from 1983 to 1996. Then coach Tony Dungy led them back to the playoffs four times from 1996 to 2001. The next year, coach Jon Gruden took them to the top.

Quarterback Steve Spurrier drops back to pass during the Buccaneers' first season in 1976.

WHO THEY PLAY

The Tampa Bay Buccaneers play 16 games each season. With so few games, each one is important. Every year, the Buccaneers play two games against each of the other three teams in their division. They are the Atlanta Falcons, the Carolina Panthers, and the New Orleans Saints. The Buccaneers have had a lot of tight battles with their division foes. Games against the other Florida teams are often intense, too. They are the Jacksonville Jaguars and the Miami Dolphins.

Buccaneers wide receiver Mike Evans (13) goes up to grab a pass against the Atlanta Falcons on November 9, 2014.

WHERE THEY PLAY

The Buccaneers first played in Tampa Stadium. Then they moved to Raymond James Stadium in 1998. That is still their home. It holds 65,890 fans. Raymond James is one of the nicest stadiums in the NFL. **Prop** makers for Disney made parts of it. This includes a large pirate ship at one end. The Buccaneers share the stadium with the University of South Florida football team. The building hosted the Super Bowl after the 2000 and 2008 seasons. It also hosts college football's Outback Bowl each year.

Fans watch the Buccaneers from the pirate ship at Raymond James Stadium.

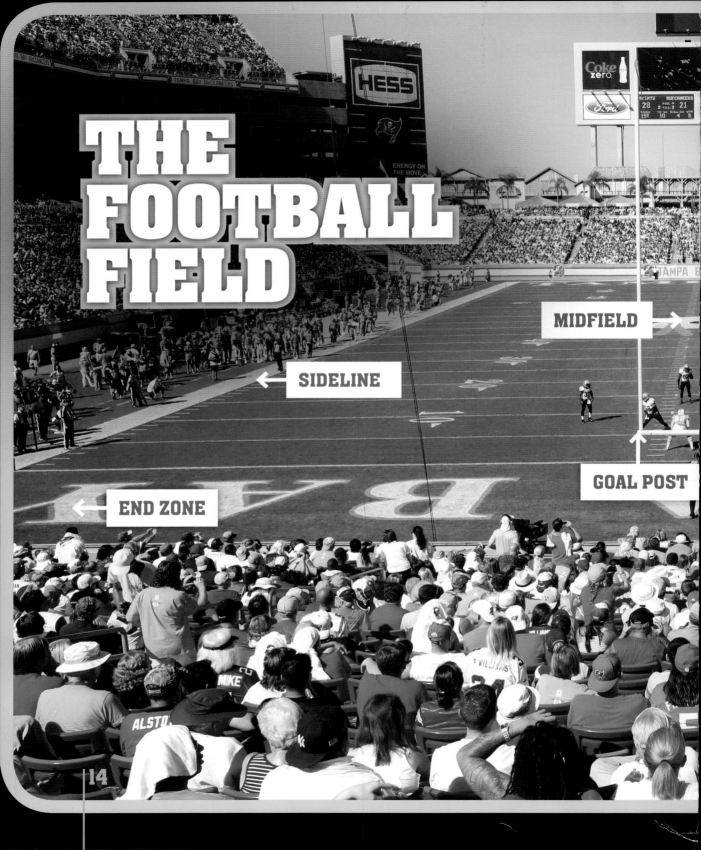

THE FOOTBALL FIELD

MIDFIELD

SIDELINE

GOAL POST

END ZONE

14

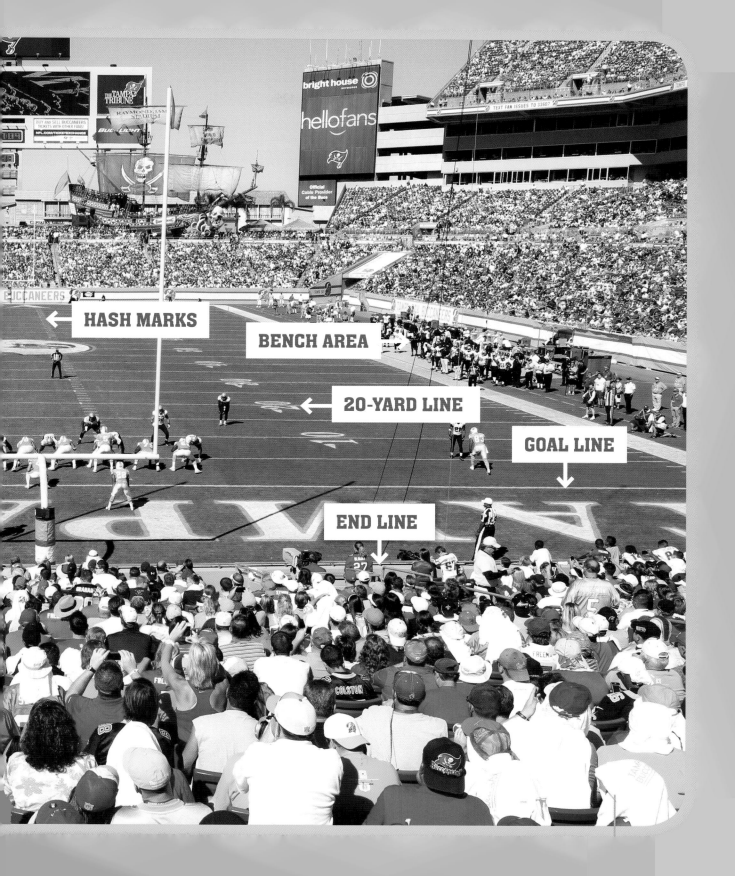

HASH MARKS

BENCH AREA

20-YARD LINE

GOAL LINE

END LINE

BIG DAYS

The Buccaneers have had some great moments in their history. Here are three of the greatest:

1977—Finally the fans could celebrate. Tampa Bay won its first home game after 13 tries. The Buccaneers beat the St. Louis Cardinals 17-7. There were 56,922 fans there. They were so happy they stormed the field and tore down the goal posts.

1995—Tampa Bay had an amazing first round of the **NFL Draft**. It selected defensive tackle Warren Sapp and linebacker Derrick Brooks on April 22. They were key players in the team's most successful seasons. Both ended up in the Pro Football Hall of Fame.

Quarterback Brad Johnson celebrates after the Buccaneers beat the Oakland Raiders in Super Bowl XXXVII on January 26, 2003.

2003—The 2002 Buccaneers rewarded their fans with a Super Bowl win. They beat the Oakland Raiders on January 26, 2003. Tampa Bay **intercepted** five Oakland passes. Buccaneers coach Jon Gruden got revenge on the Raiders. He had coached them from 1998 to 2001.

TOUGH DAYS

Football is a hard game. Even the best teams have rough games and seasons. Here are some of the toughest times in Buccaneers history:

1976—Tampa Bay fans were happy to have a football team. But they did not have much to cheer about that first season. The Buccaneers went 0-14. They were **shut out** five times. No other NFL team went winless in a season until the 2008 Detroit Lions.

1987—Tampa Bay had gone 3-16 in games started by quarterback Steve Young from 1985 to 1986. So they traded him to the San Francisco 49ers on April 25. Young became a superstar. He won two NFL **Most Valuable Player (MVP)** awards and the Super Bowl with San Francisco.

Buccaneers running back Ed Williams is tackled by an Oakland Raiders player during a game on November 28, 1976.

1999—It was a bad day for the Buccaneers. They lost 45-0 to the Oakland Raiders on December 19. It is still one of the worst losses in team history. Tampa Bay allowed 262 rushing yards.

MEET THE FANS

Tampa Bay fans have supported their team even in bad times. Some of them show up to games wearing crazy pirate gear. Buccaneers fans love the large pirate ship in Raymond James Stadium. It shoots cannons when the home team scores. Mascot Captain Fear is said to live in the ship. He first appeared in 2000.

Fans cheer on the Buccaneers during a 2014 game at Raymond James Stadium.

HEROES THEN

Coaches Tony Dungy and Jon Gruden led the most successful Tampa Bay seasons. They combined to lead from 1996 to 2008. The Buccaneers were in the top ten in scoring **defense** each of those seasons except one. Warren Sapp and Derrick Brooks often led that dominant defense. Cornerback Ronde Barber was a force, too. He played in Tampa Bay his whole career, from 1997 to 2012. Running back James Wilder played for the Buccaneers in the 1980s. He was a workhorse who was great at both rushing and catching the ball.

Buccaneers linebacker Derrick Brooks returns an interception for a touchdown in Super Bowl XXXVII on January 26, 2003.

HEROES NOW

Defensive tackle Gerald McCoy is keeping the Buccaneers defensive tradition strong. He was selected third overall in the 2010 NFL Draft. McCoy made the **Pro Bowl** in 2012, 2013, and 2014. Linebacker Lavonte David was drafted in 2012. He has been a starter since then. He was named an All-Pro in 2013. Wide receivers Mike Evans and Vincent Jackson are tall and strong. They use their height and strength to make exciting catches.

The Buccaneers' Gerald McCoy blasts through the Carolina Panthers' offensive line on December 1, 2013.

GEARING UP

NFL players wear team uniforms. They wear helmets and pads to keep them safe. Cleats help them make quick moves and run fast. Some players wear extra gear for protection.

THE FOOTBALL

NFL footballs are made of leather. Under the leather is a lining that fills with air to give the ball its shape. The leather has bumps, or "pebbles." These help players grip the ball. Laces help players control their throws. Footballs are also called "pigskins" because some of the first balls were made from pig bladders. Today, they are made of leather from cows.

Wide receiver Mike Evans runs with the ball during a game against the Atlanta Falcons on November 9, 2014.

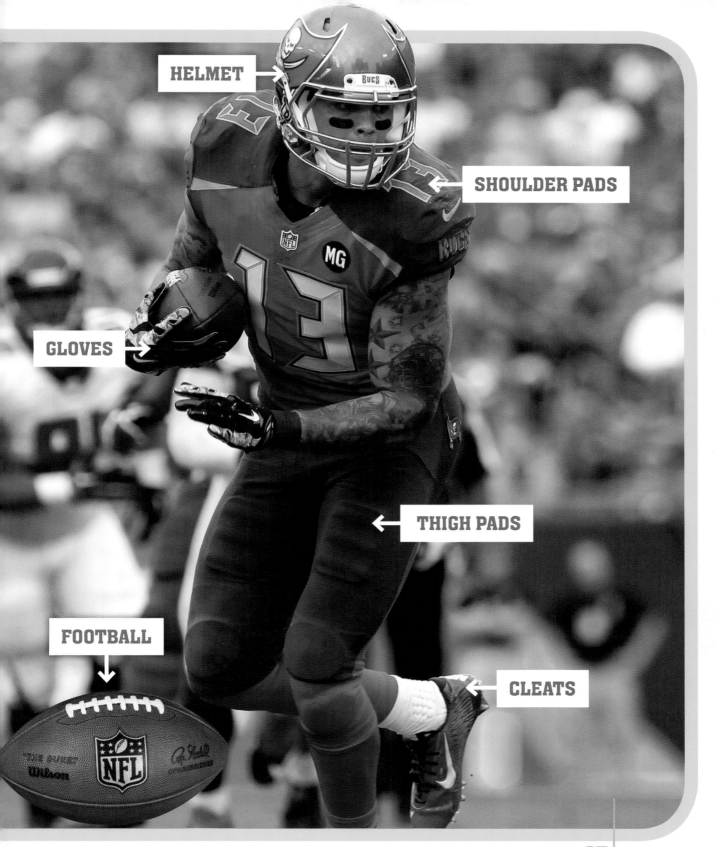

HELMET

SHOULDER PADS

GLOVES

THIGH PADS

FOOTBALL

CLEATS

SPORTS STATS

 Here are some of the all-time career records for the Tampa Bay Buccaneers. All the stats are through the 2014 season.

PASSING YARDS

Vinny Testaverde 14,820

Josh Freeman 13,534

RUSHING YARDS

James Wilder 5,957

Mike Alstott 5,088

RECEPTIONS

James Wilder 430

Mark Carrier 321

TOTAL TOUCHDOWNS

Mike Alstott 71

James Wilder 46

SACKS

Warren Sapp 77.0

Simeon Rice 69.5

POINTS

Martin Gramatica 592

Michael Husted 502

Buccaneers cornerback Ronde Barber runs an interception back for a touchdown during a 2000 game against the New York Jets.

INTERCEPTIONS

Ronde Barber 47

Donnie Abraham 31

GLOSSARY

defense when a team doesn't have the ball and is trying to keep the other team from scoring

intercepted when a player on the defense catches a forward pass

league an organization of sports teams that compete against each other

Most Valuable Player (MVP) a yearly award given to the top player in the NFL

NFL Draft a meeting of all the NFL teams at which they choose college players to join them

Pro Bowl the NFL's all-star game, in which the best players in the league compete

prop something used to create the setting in a movie or play

shut out when a team scores zero points

Super Bowl the championship game of the NFL, played between the winners of the AFC and the NFC

FIND OUT MORE

IN THE LIBRARY

Editors of Sports Illustrated Kids. *Sports Illustrated Kids Football: Then to WOW!*
New York: Time Home Entertainment, 2014.

Frisch, Nate. *The Story of the Tampa Bay Buccaneers.*
Mankato, MN: Creative Education, 2014.

ON THE WEB

Visit our Web site for links about the Tampa Bay Buccaneers:
childsworld.com/links

Note to Parents, Teachers, and Librarians: We routinely verify our Web links to make sure they are safe and active sites. So encourage your readers to check them out!

INDEX